A Wild Ride on the WATER CYCLE

A Jake & Alice Adventure

For my wife, Rebecca, and the real Jake and Alice—
Amber, Abby & Jacob

bright sky press
HOUSTON, TEXAS

2365 Rice Blvd., Suite 202
Houston, Texas 77005

ISBN: 978-1-939055-80-4

10 9 8 7 6 5 4 3 2 1

Library of Congress Cataloging-in-Publication Data on file with publisher.

Editorial Direction, Lucy Herring Chambers
Editor, Eva J. Freeburn
Design, Marla Y. Garcia

Production Date: October 2014
Plant & Location: Printed by We SP Corp., Seoul, Korea
Job/Batch #: 42671-0

WATER CYCLE

A Wild Ride on the

A Jake & Alice Adventure

ANTHONY YANEZ

Illustrations by MIKE GUILLORY

bright sky press

HOUSTON, TEXAS

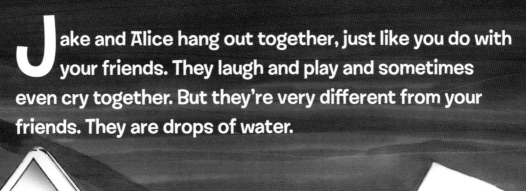

Jake and Alice hang out together, just like you do with your friends. They laugh and play and sometimes even cry together. But they're very different from your friends. They are drops of water.

A water molecule is made up of two hydrogen atoms and one oxygen atom: H_2O.

Jake and Alice met in a lake, so long ago there were still dinosaurs in the water and on the land. Jake, who is shy and quiet, saw these strange creatures all around. When he noticed Alice, who is brave and adventurous, splashing near the shore, he swam over to her. He didn't feel so alone anymore.

"Nice to meet you," said Alice. "Don't fret. They look tough, but they won't hurt you."

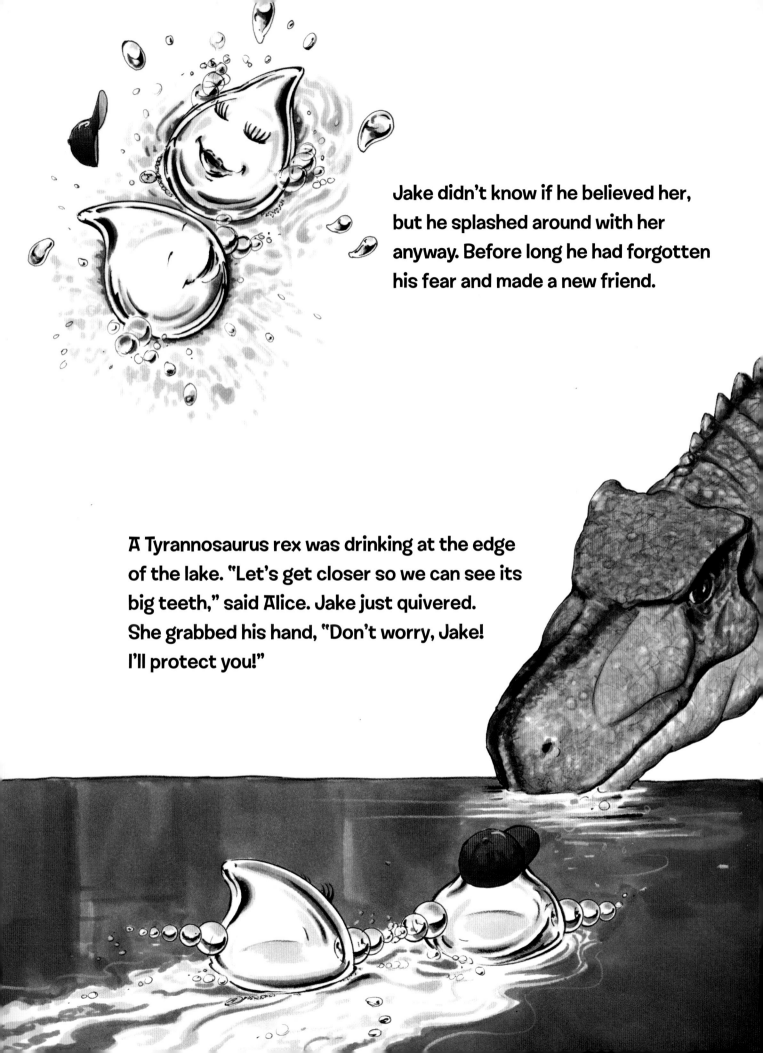

Jake didn't know if he believed her, but he splashed around with her anyway. Before long he had forgotten his fear and made a new friend.

A Tyrannosaurus rex was drinking at the edge of the lake. "Let's get closer so we can see its big teeth," said Alice. Jake just quivered. She grabbed his hand, "Don't worry, Jake! I'll protect you!"

They drifted closer, and the dinosaur
swallowed the two friends whole!

"Whoa! What's happening?" They shouted as they
slipped and slid down the dinosaur's long throat.
When they finally landed in his stomach, it was pitch
black. "I guess that wasn't such a good idea," said Alice.

They stayed close to each other in the dark, so it wasn't
scary. But with no sunlight, their days began to run together.

They sloshed around, telling jokes and stories,
until one day their whole world shook.

The mighty dinosaur fell to the
ground and died.

When any living thing dies, the earth absorbs the water inside the body. Jake and Alice were pulled from the blackness of the dinosaur into the warm brown of the earth. Plant and tree roots surrounded them like a spider's web. Jake got scared again. "Don't worry, Jake," said Alice. "I'm here. I won't leave you." Jake remembered how she had gotten them swallowed by the T-rex; but he knew she was a good friend, so he didn't say anything.

Like all living things, plants and trees need water to survive. Water drops carry vital nutrients to vegetation. Alice held Jake's hand as a tree root drew them in for nourishment.

From the root they traveled up the tall trunk, out on a limb and into the veins of a leaf. Everything looked bright and green, and the two friends swayed gently in the breeze. They relaxed, feeling the warmth of the sun.

As the temperatures warmed, Jake and Alice began to feel funny. Suddenly, they felt themselves floating away. "Alice, where are you? I can't see you!" called Jake.

"I'm right here, Jake! But, where are you?"

The friends had transformed from liquid water into invisible water vapor. They were in danger of losing each other. Now they were both scared.

Alice grasped around in the air until she found Jake's hand. "I've got you!" She grabbed him just in time.

After extracting the nutrients from water, the leaves **TRANSPIRE** excess water back into the atmosphere. Think of it as plants sweating.

What started out as a slow ascent quickly turned into a race upward. They felt like they were in a rocket launching into space. They were caught in an updraft, a part of a storm that brings moisture from the ground to the very top of the clouds. As they climbed higher and higher, the temperature got colder. Jake and Alice began to shiver, and then to freeze. Their bodies started to collect ice.

The ice built up until they were in the center of a baseball-sized piece of hail. Once they reached the top of the cloud, they shot back to the earth at 100 miles per hour. It was a wild ride!

On the ground, Jake and Alice melted quickly. The sun shone on them, evaporating them for the second time. "Oh, no! Here we go again!" Alice said.

Hail can form in any month with the peak activity in April and May. A typical hail storm lasts twenty minutes.

WATER VAPOR rises because it is lighter than most other atmospheric gases.

This time they didn't rise nearly as fast or travel as far. They turned from invisible water vapor to drops of rain and fell, landing with a splash into a river.

Now Jake was getting used to the adventure. "This is fun, Alice!" he called, as they raced down the rushing river.

When they slowed down, they found themselves in a huge ocean. This body of water would be their home for a long time.

RUNOFF is when water is moved from lakes or rivers into the ocean.

For many years, Jake and Alice explored the seas. They swam through all of the oceans of the world. They played with dolphins and whales in the Pacific, saw colorful coral reefs near Australia, and even hung out with penguins in the Antarctic.

If the Antarctic ice cap were melted it would yield enough fresh water to supply all of the rivers of the world for 750 years.

Their journey took 2,000 years. It didn't seem very long to Jake and Alice. They were best friends now. They splashed happily around the world, talking endlessly about the fascinating sights along the way.

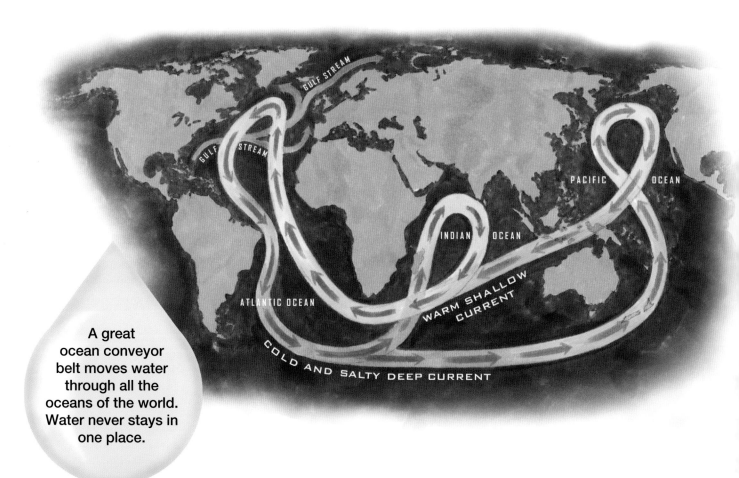

A great ocean conveyor belt moves water through all the oceans of the world. Water never stays in one place.

One especially hot summer day in the Atlantic Ocean, Alice noticed thunderstorms a short distance away. She was experienced enough by now to know that soon she and Jake would become water vapor again and begin the journey to the sky. She wasn't worried.

CONDENSATION
When water is evaporated, it condenses into clouds, which are extremely small water drops.

This time it was different. As Jake and Alice rocketed up, they condensed into a raging swirl of clouds. It was loud, windy, and scary.

"Stay together!" Alice shouted.

"What?" Jake called, spinning away from her.

Alice caught Jake's hand just as the clouds started to circle the eye of the storm.

Water cannot disappear or die. It will always exist as liquid water, ice, or vapor.

As the storm moved into the Gulf of Mexico, Jake and Alice's speed picked up. They held on for dear life as the winds around the center of the hurricane twisted at 125 miles per hour.

Jake thought his life was over.

Finally, the hurricane made landfall on Galveston Island in Texas.

Jake and Alice turned from a spinning cloud into huge rain drops. Friction and gravity flatten all rain drops, so they fell to the ground shaped like hamburgers! This wasn't a gentle rain shower—it was a torrential downpour.

Jake and Alice were a part of a powerful flood that damaged homes and cars and uprooted trees. "Oh, no!" said Alice. "Did we do this?"

Hurricane season is from June 1st to November 30th. These monster storms form when ocean water that is at least 150 feet deep reaches 80° F.

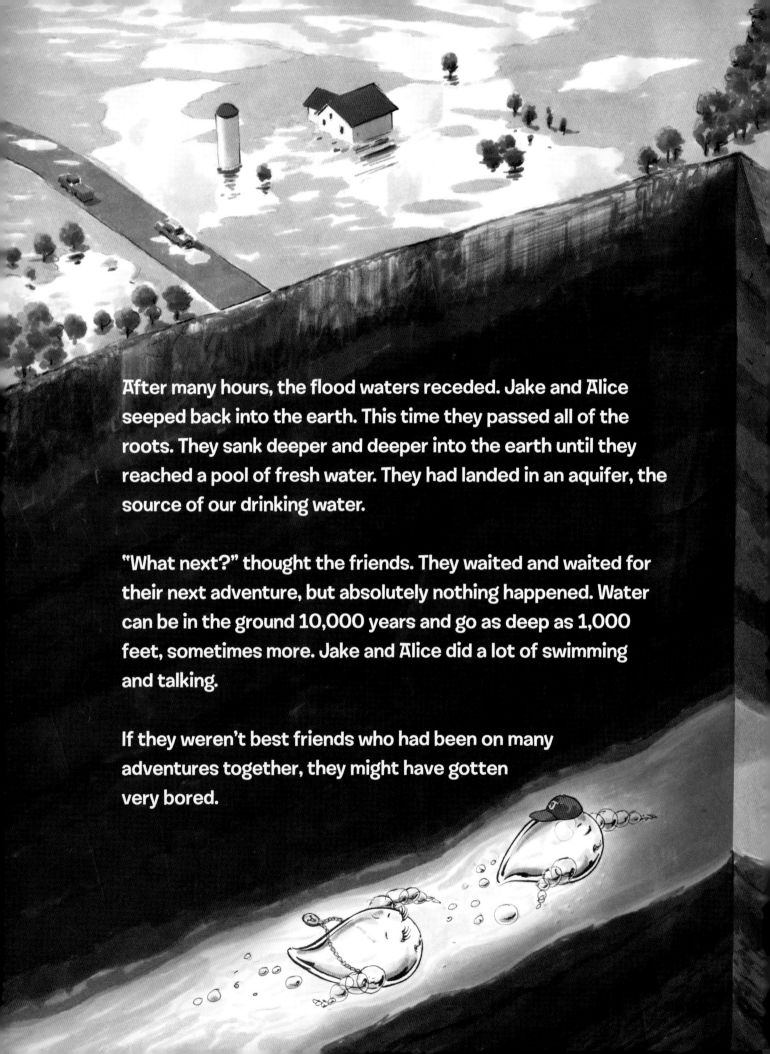

After many hours, the flood waters receded. Jake and Alice seeped back into the earth. This time they passed all of the roots. They sank deeper and deeper into the earth until they reached a pool of fresh water. They had landed in an aquifer, the source of our drinking water.

"What next?" thought the friends. They waited and waited for their next adventure, but absolutely nothing happened. Water can be in the ground 10,000 years and go as deep as 1,000 feet, sometimes more. Jake and Alice did a lot of swimming and talking.

If they weren't best friends who had been on many adventures together, they might have gotten very bored.

It seemed to take an eternity, but Jake and Alice finally climbed up to the surface of the earth. Underground pipes pulled them into a kitchen refrigerator freezer.

BELLAIRE LITTLE LEAGUE WORLD SERIES CHAMPS

Half of our drinking water in the United States, about 12 million gallons per day, comes from **GROUND WATER.**

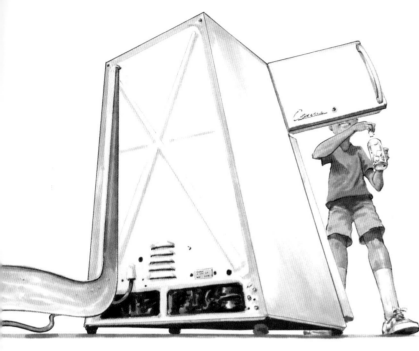

"I-i-i-t's c-c-cold in here! Where are we?" Jake whispered as his teeth chattered. They turned from water to a frozen cube of ice. It was the coldest they had ever been. Even hugs couldn't warm them up.

Too cold to even talk, they stayed in the dark freezer for a few days. Finally, the freezer door opened and the light went on. A boy named Tom reached in and scooped them up. He put them in a glass of water. Jake and Alice began to melt. The boy put the cup up to his mouth. "Not again!" said Jake.

Alice laughed. "I wonder if he knows he's drinking the same water that a dinosaur drank?" Jake laughed too. Down the hatch they went. It was just as dark as it had been in the T-rex.

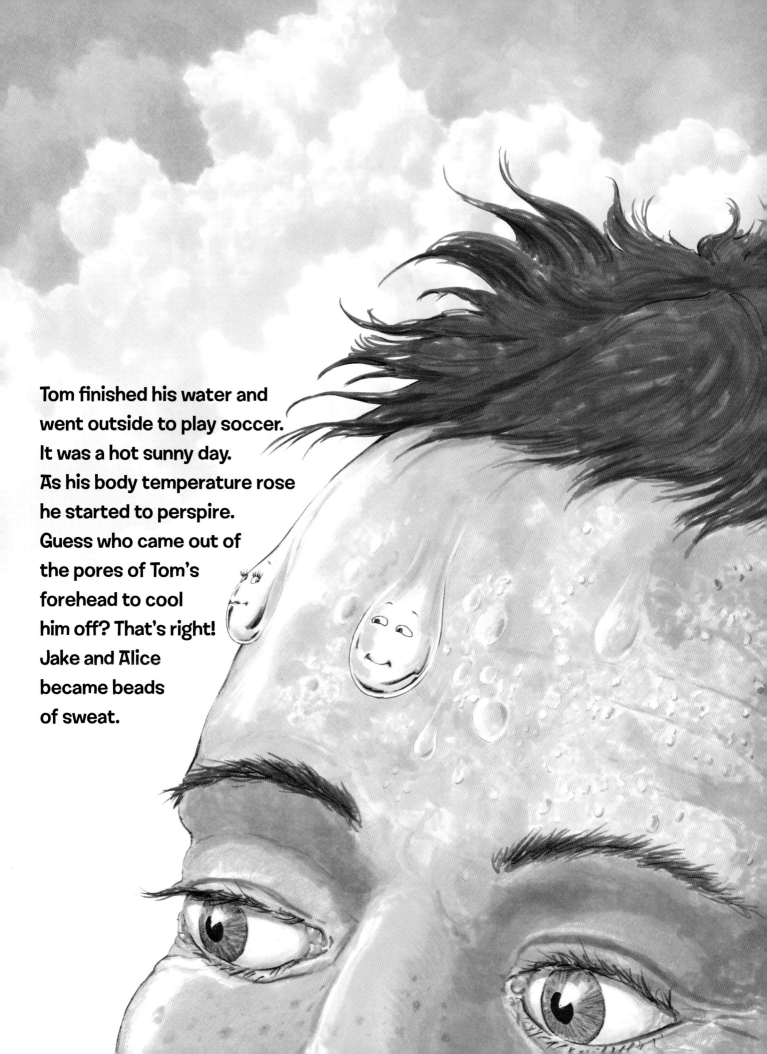

Tom finished his water and
went outside to play soccer.
It was a hot sunny day.
As his body temperature rose
he started to perspire.
Guess who came out of
the pores of Tom's
forehead to cool
him off? That's right!
Jake and Alice
became beads
of sweat.

The sun's solar energy is the main power source driving the water cycle.

They soon evaporated off Tom's skin. They rose gently into the sky and became a small part of a beautiful, puffy cumulus cloud. The clouds provided shade to Tom and his friends who played beneath them.

Jake and Alice floated gently above the United States as clouds. On nice days they transformed into cirrus clouds, soaring 30,000 feet above the earth.

In San Antonio, Texas, they hugged the ground as fog, which is a stratus cloud that forms on the earth's surface.

They saw stunning mountain peaks, and the view of the ocean from up in the sky was breathtaking.

As summer turned to fall, and fall to winter, the beautiful colors below them faded and the temperature got cold again. Jake and Alice started falling from the cloud.

There are three main types of clouds: **CIRRUS, CUMULUS,** and **STRATUS.** Cirrus is the highest, cumulus are in the middle, and stratus are low clouds.

As Jake looked at his friend, he realized she had never looked so beautiful. They had become snowflakes, gliding silently to the ground.

They landed on a frozen lake in Thunder Bay, Ontario, Canada. Ice skaters enjoyed the winter, laughing and swirling around the ice. Jake and Alice loved watching the skaters. The friends had become part of the ice, so they had a very good view.

Like finger prints, snowflakes, are all unique. No two flakes are the same.

Three months later, as winter turned to spring, the friends melted into the lake. Looking around, Jake realized they had returned to the spot where they had met, all those years ago.

There were even creatures drinking off the shore, but none were as big as the dinosaurs. Alice clutched Jake's hand. "Let's stay in the middle and swim for awhile," she said. "It's much safer here."

Jake laughed and splashed her. "Aren't you ready to take another wild ride? Don't worry, Alice. I'll protect you!"

The water cycle involves: evaporation, condensation, precipitation, infiltration, evapotranspiration, ground water and runoff. Can you find where Jake and Alice go through each of these stages in the story?

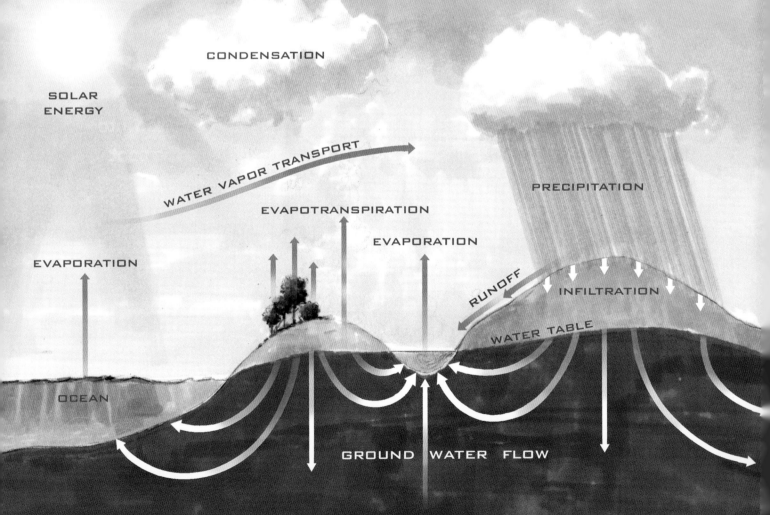

CONDENSATION

SOLAR ENERGY

WATER VAPOR TRANSPORT

EVAPOTRANSPIRATION

EVAPORATION

PRECIPITATION

EVAPORATION

RUNOFF

INFILTRATION

WATER TABLE

OCEAN

GROUND WATER FLOW

GLOSSARY

EVAPORATION – The change from liquid to gas.

CONDENSATION – The change from gas to liquid.

PRECIPITATION – Water that falls to Earth, such as drizzle, rain, ice pellets, snow, hail.

INFILTRATION – The flow of water from the ground surface down into the soil.

EVAPOTRANSPIRATION – The process that returns moisture to the atmosphere through vegetation.

GROUND WATER – Water beneath the land surface.

RUNOFF – Raindrops that fall to Earth and travel to the nearest stream, lake or ocean.